Little Stinker

By Stephen Sanzo

Illustrated by Mark Mullaney
(based on the art of Matt Whitlock)

Cranky Pants Publishing

A Special Thank You

This book would not have been possible if not for the support of these great folks:

Bob and Jan Sanzo
Chris Sanzo and Roberta Groch
Michael and Kim Gruber
Rubin and Cindy Gruber
The Kickstarter supporters

Copyright © 2013 by Stephen Sanzo

Published by Cranky Pants Publishing, LLC, Arlington, MA
Cranky Pants Publishing is distributed to the trade by AtlasBooks

ISBN 978-0-9759627-1-8
Library of Congress Control Number: 2013913019

Printed in the United States

First Edition
1 3 5 7 9 10 8 6 4 2

www.crankypantspublishing.com

This is my sister.

I call her the Little Stinker.

She gets up at five o'clock every morning,

stomps in her crib,

and honks like a goose.

When I am at school, the Little Stinker steals my G.I. Joe with Kung-Fu Grip, puts him in PINK dresses, and sits him at her tea parties.

She takes my favorite
cowboy boots, hides
in Mom's closet,
and plays with
all the shoes.

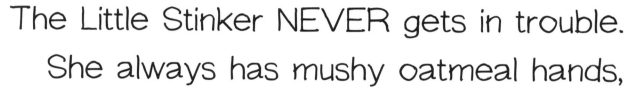

The Little Stinker NEVER gets in trouble.
She always has mushy oatmeal hands,
sticky grape jelly hair,
a runny nose,
and smelly feet.

We are going shopping today.

Maybe if I am really, really good Mom and Dad will buy me the new Sting-Ray bike with super fast tires, rear shocks, and a stick shift!

Mom and Dad help the Little Stinker put on her jacket and sneakers. I wish they would hurry up.

I don't need any help.
I can do it myself.

The Little Stinker yells, "GROOOOOOOOVY!" the whole ride in the car. She always says that. Mom and Dad think it's funny.

I ignore the Stinker and talk about how cool it would be if I had the new Sting-Ray bike.

The Little Stinker stops
to pick up leaves . . .

and wave at people . . .

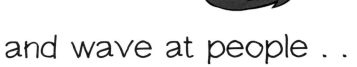

and lick the pavement.

She is the slowest
walker ever.

The store
is HUGE.

Mom takes the Little Stinker to try on dresses. I go with Dad to look at TVs.

FINALLY, we make it to the toys.
The Little Stinker screams, "Mine! Mine!
GROOOVVY!" at everything she sees.

We don't even look at bikes. Mom and Dad pick out a game for me to share with the Stinker.

I don't want to share
with the Little Stinker.

I don't want to play
with the Little Stinker.

I would like her to move
to Grandma's house.

My mom makes me hold the Stinker's
hand AGAIN while we wait in line.

I turn around to look at the coolest bike ever.
The STING-RAY!

Oh no!
Where did the
Little Stinker go?

We look under the dress racks and behind the TVs.

We even ask the scary lady
at the lay-away desk.

Are there
MONSTERS in this store!?

What if we don't find the Little Stinker?

Who will I throw snowballs at?

Who will I scare when I jump out of the closet?

Who will show
her how to color
in the lines?

Who will help her tie her shoes . . . ?

That's it!

"GROOOVVY!"

I am very happy to see the Little Stinker.

The man in the shoe department is happy to see her leave.

The Little Stinker holds on tight to my hand
as we walk out of the store.

I don't mind at all.